WELCOME TO

RAVENS PASS

NEW IN TOWN

Ravens Pass is published by Stone Arch Books
a Capstone imprint
1710 Roe Crest Drive
North Mankato, Minnesota 56003
www.capstonepub.com

Library of Congress Cataloging-in-Publication Data
Brezenoff, Steven.
New in town / written by Steve Brezenoff ; illustrated by Tom Percival.

p. cm. -- (Ravens Pass)

Summary: Jake Demby is being bullied by a kid called Gary Herk, until his friend sends him a golem named Emmet from Ravens Pass as a protector--but when Emmet threatens Jake's mother the situation starts to spin out of control.

ISBN 978-1-4342-3793-4 (library binding) -- ISBN 978-1-4342-4210-5 (pbk.) -- ISBN 978-1-4342-4653-0 (ebook)

1. Golem--Juvenile fiction. 2. Bullying--Juvenile fiction. 3. Paranormal fiction. 4. Horror tales. [1. Golem--Fiction. 2. Supernatural--Fiction. 3. Bullies--Fiction. 4. Horror stories.] I. Percival, Tom, 1977- ill. II. Title.

PZ7.B7576Ne 2012
[Fic]--dc23

2012003960

Graphic Designer: Hilary Wacholz
Art Director: Kay Fraser

Photo credits:
iStockphoto: chromatika (sign, backcover); spxChrome (torn paper, pp. 7, 15, 23, 31, 39, 47, 53, 65, 75, 83)
Shutterstock: Milos Luzanin (newspaper, pp. 92, 93, 94, 95, 96); Robyn Mackenzie (torn ad, pp. 1, 2, 96); Tischenko Irina (sign, p. 1, 2); Alan49 (trees, pp.25). Photographic textures and elements from cgtextures, composited by Tom Percival: (front cover and pp. 9, 12-13, 18, 25, 35, 44, 49, 59, 71, 78, 84, 87, 93)

Printed in the United States of America
in Stevens Point, Wisconsin.
042012   006678WZF12

Between where you live and where you've been, there is a town. It lies along the highway, and off the beaten path. It's in the middle of a forest, and in the middle of a desert. It's on the shore of a lake, and along a raging river. It's surrounded by mountains, and on the edge of a deadly cliff. If you're looking for it, you'll never find it, but if you're lost, it'll appear on your path.

The town is **RAVENS PASS**, and you might never leave.

TABLE OF CONTENTS

Chapter 1

BULLY

Andy Demby used the back of his hand to wipe the mud out of his eyes. He didn't bother clearing the mud from his ears just yet. It helped to muffle the laughter of the three boys standing over him.

He felt around for his glasses and found them nearby. They were pretty bent, but he managed to get them on.

"Are you done?" he asked.

He rolled onto his side in the mud puddle and looked up at Gary Burk.

Gary was the lead bully.

Gary chuckled once. Then he snarled. "For now," he said. "But we'll see you again real soon."

The other two goons laughed. Then all three bullies walked off.

Andy got to his feet. He found his books in the trashcan nearby. He cleaned them as best as he could and slipped them back into his book bag.

For all of sixth grade, Gary Burk and his friends had picked on Andy and his best and only friend, Scott Stevens. But this summer, Scott's family moved to Ravens Pass, a small town all the way on the other end of the county.

Now it was the first day of seventh grade, and Andy was the only one left for Gary and his friends to pick on.

It was kind of weird. Gary Burk had moved to Andy's town from Ravens Pass a year earlier. Even weirder, Scott and Andy used to pick on one of Gary's friends, Evan, before Gary moved to town.

Boy, did Andy regret ever picking on that guy. He was sure Evan was the one who got Gary to pick on them.

Andy started walking up the front steps of Blue Sky Middle School. "Well," he muttered, "seventh grade seems a lot like sixth grade so far."

The first bell rang through the empty halls. Andy trudged in his muddied shoes toward homeroom. "Except this year," Andy said to himself, "I'm facing Gary Burk on my own."

* * *

"Here," Andy said in homeroom. He put up his hand and waved vigorously. He'd noticed in the past that sometimes teachers had trouble seeing him if he didn't wave a lot and say "here" as loud as he could.

The teacher, Mr. Dunn, smiled at him and nodded. "I see you," he said. "Thank you."

Andy felt a slap across the back of his head. "Ow!" he said.

"What was that?" Mr. Dunn asked.

"Um, nothing," Andy said, rubbing the back of his head. "Sorry."

Mr. Dunn went on with the attendance. Andy turned around in his seat. Gary Burk was sitting behind him.

"Oh, it's you," Andy said. "Great."

"Yup," Gary said. "And these are our assigned seats. I'll be sitting behind you all year." He laced his fingers together and cracked his knuckles.

Andy faced forward and his shoulders drooped. Seventh grade would be a very long year.

Chapter 2
THE NEW KID

Andy managed to avoid Gary and his bully friends for the rest of the day. He made sure to get a seat in the back row of all his classes. He ate alone in the cafeteria, at a small table hidden behind a brick column where no one could see him.

When last hour ended, Andy took his time packing up his stuff. He wanted the halls to be empty of everyone—especially Gary Burk and his buddies. By the time he got to the front doors of the school, he thought he was safe.

The halls were empty, all right. But out front, trouble was waiting.

"There he is," Gary said as Andy walked down the front steps. "We've been waiting for you."

Andy stopped walking. There was no escape. When this happened last year, Scott would go one way, and Andy would go the other. If they ran as fast they could, one of them would always get away. Sometimes both would escape without getting tossed in the mud, or dropped headfirst into a trashcan.

But now Andy was alone. If he ran, all three bullies would chase him. They'd catch him eventually. He decided not to bother.

"Well, here I am," Andy said. He held out his book bag. "Take my bag, toss it in the mud. Whatever. Just get it over with."

Gary walked slowly toward him. "Now, that's no fun, Andy," Gary said. His two friends fell in line behind Gary. The three bullies stood at the bottom of the steps and smirked up at Andy.

Andy swallowed hard. He took a deep breath. Then he walked down the steps, right at Gary.

The henchmen each took one of Andy's arms and held him. Gary smiled at Andy.

"Time to take your punishment, Andy," Gary said.

"Punishment for what?" Andy asked.

Gary shrugged. "I don't know," he said. He thought for a second and smirked, then said, "For being so short."

Then he pulled back his fist and punched Andy right in the gut.

Andy fell to his knees. The henchmen laughed. They let go of his arms, and Andy fell forward into the mud at the bottom of the steps. He could tell that his glasses were getting bent even more.

"Now, where have I seen this before?" Gary asked, pretending to be confused. His friends laughed.

"Hand me his bag," Gary said. Then he suddenly screamed, "Hey, get off—"

Andy rolled onto his side and looked up. The afternoon sun was bright, and Andy had to squint to see. Gary Burk was a foot off the ground, his arms and legs waving wildly and helplessly.

"Let go of me!" he shouted.

His henchmen just watched, mouths wide open.

Then Gary fell in a heap, right into the mud, next to Andy.

Standing there, with his back to the sun, was a boy Andy had never seen before. He was taller than Gary, broader than Gary, and apparently stronger than Gary. With the sun behind the tall stranger, it was too hard for Andy to see his face.

The stranger leaned down and put out his hand. Andy grabbed it and stood up.

The henchmen exchanged a look, and then ran off. Gary slowly got to his feet. "Wait for me," he called after his friends. Then he jogged after them, shooting nervous looks back at Andy and the strange kid.

Andy watched the three bullies run off. Then he turned to the stranger.

"Who are you?" Andy asked.

"I'm Emmet," the stranger said. "I'm new here."

Chapter 3

A GIFT

"That was so cool!" Andy said. He and Emmet walked along Grove Street, toward Andy's house. "The way you picked up that jerk Gary," Andy went on, "he must have felt so dumb."

Emmet didn't say anything. He just kept walking.

Andy's smile, which had been huge for the last two blocks, faded just a little. "So, do you live in this neighborhood too?" Andy asked.

"Yes," Emmet said.

Andy waited for him to say more. When he didn't, Andy added, "I live on Dell Circle. What about you?"

Emmet coughed. He looked around quickly, and then said, "I live on Grove Street."

Andy stopped. "Oh, did we already pass your house?" he asked.

"Yes," Emmet said. "But it doesn't matter. I will turn around after you are home."

"Okay," Andy said. "You're my personal bodyguard, huh?" He laughed.

Emmet did not even smile.

"So you're new?" Andy asked.

Emmet nodded.

"Where are you from?" Andy asked.

Emmet looked down at Andy for a moment. "Ravens Pass," he said.

"No kidding?" Andy said. "My friend moved to Ravens Pass a couple of weeks ago. His name is Scott Stevens. Do you know him?"

"No," Emmet said.

Andy shrugged. "Oh well," he said. "He probably got to Ravens Pass just as your family was moving away."

Emmet walked on. He kept his eyes on the horizon.

When they reached Dell Circle, Andy stopped. "This is my street," he said. He pointed at a blue house. "That's my house."

"All right," Emmet said. He turned around to walk back down Grove Street.

"Um, bye," Andy said. "I'll see you at school, right?"

Emmet didn't reply. He just walked on.

* * *

At home, Andy said hi to his mom and ducked into the family room. He turned on the computer and checked his messages.

He only had one. It was from his old best friend, Scott Stevens.

Scott seemed to be getting along great in Ravens Pass. He already had a bunch of good friends, and today was only the first day of school.

Andy sighed.

"How did he make friends so quickly?" Andy muttered. "Meanwhile I'm stuck with Gary and those jerks." He sighed. "At least I've got Emmet now," he said.

He pictured the tall new kid's unsmiling face. "I mean, I think he's my friend," he added to himself, smiling. "Who knows."

The last line of Scott's message read, "Did you get the gift I sent you?"

Andy looked around, but he didn't see any packages. He called into the living room, "Mom, did anything come in the mail for me today, from Scott?"

"No," his mom called back. "Are you expecting something? Do you want me to call his mom and ask?"

"No, that's okay. It'll probably get here tomorrow," Andy said. "Don't worry about it."

Chapter 4

SAVED AGAIN

The next morning, Andy approached the school slowly. He wanted to make sure Gary and his friends weren't waiting for him. They'd probably want revenge after Gary ended up in the mud. So if the three bullies were waiting, Andy would have to make sure Emmet was waiting, too.

Andy stopped on the edge of the middle school grounds. He stood behind the big oak tree at the corner and peeked around.

"There they are," he muttered to himself.

Gary and his two bully friends were leaning on the railing at the front steps. They were obviously waiting for Andy. He knew they'd want to teach him a lesson.

Andy scanned the schoolyard. He didn't see Emmet anywhere. If the big new kid didn't show up soon . . . well, Andy didn't even want to think about what the bullies would do today.

He leaned his back against the big tree. Maybe if he waited long enough, the bullies would give up and go inside.

He strained to listen for the first bell. He heard other students laughing and shouting. He saw a few kids, running late, jog past him as they headed toward the school.

Suddenly, a strong hand fell onto his shoulder. Andy spun around. "Emmet!" he said.

The big new kid looked down at him and nodded.

"I'm glad to see you," Andy said. "Gary and his goons are waiting for me. They must be pretty mad about yesterday."

Emmet looked toward the front of the school. "I see," he said. "Let's go."

He didn't wait for a reply. He just started walking toward the front of the school.

Andy stayed a few paces behind the taller boy, but he couldn't have kept up even if he'd wanted to. Emmet's long legs were like tree trunks stomping quickly and heavily across the school's front lawn.

As Emmet approached, Gary and his friends stood up straighter.

Gary moved to block the steps. His friends followed and stood on each side of him. "Well, well," Gary said. He smirked. "If it isn't Andy and his personal oaf."

"You're pretty confident, aren't you?" Andy said, still a few feet behind Emmet. "I mean, after what happened yesterday, what makes you think you can talk to us like that?"

Gary frowned and said, "He snuck up behind me. Now he'll pay. And so will you, Andy, so don't go anywhere."

Emmet took a heavy step toward Gary. Gary's bully friends flinched, but no one ran off.

Emmet took another step.

"Get him!" Gary shouted. He and his friends charged at Emmet. They wrapped their arms around him to tackle him.

Emmet didn't budge.

Gary moved around and leaped onto Emmet's back. His goons pounded on Emmet's stomach and chest.

Emmet didn't flinch.

Finally, the new kid had had enough. With a great bellow, he threw out his arms, sending Gary and his friends flying and tumbling into the thick mud.

The three bullies slowly got to their feet. Gary shook his head to clear it. "This isn't over," he said. "We'll get you back for this."

The three bullies ran off. The first bell rang.

"Oh no," Andy said. "I'm going to be late for homeroom again."

Emmet didn't move. He just stood there, watching the three bullies as they ran.

"Thanks," Andy said. He hurried up the steps and opened the school's front door. Emmet didn't follow.

"Aren't you going to homeroom?" Andy asked.

Emmet squinted at Andy. "Not right now," Emmet said. "I will go later."

Andy laughed. Emmet didn't.

"Okay, well, I'll see you," Andy said. He headed to class.

Chapter 5

NOT MY BUSINESS

After last bell that afternoon, Andy walked quickly through the halls. He wanted to find Emmet as soon as he could. He didn't want to face Gary and the goons on his own.

Sure enough, as soon as he stepped outside, Emmet was there.

"Hey," Andy said. "You weren't in school today at all."

"Maybe you just didn't see me," Emmet said. He started walking, and Andy followed.

"Huh. That would be weird," Andy said. "You're not exactly easy to miss."

Andy and Emmet walked quietly down Grove Street for a block or so. Once in a while, Andy stole a glance at Emmet. The kid was a total mystery, but if he was against the bullies, he was okay with Andy.

Suddenly Andy heard a scream from the small park at the corner of Pine Place. He stopped and grabbed Emmet's wrist.

"Look," Andy said. He pointed at the park.

Gary and his friends were there, standing in a cluster with their backs to him and Emmet. They were laughing. But none of them had made the scream Andy had heard. He was almost positive that it had sounded like a girl.

"Come on," Andy said. He jogged across the intersection toward the park. "Hey," he called.

Gary and his friends turned to watch Andy coming. They stepped apart just enough that Andy could see a girl sitting in the mud. That's who had screamed: their latest victim.

Andy muttered over his shoulder, "Teach those jerks a lesson." Emmet didn't reply. Andy added, "Come on, Emmet. Stop Gary and his friends from picking on that girl."

Emmet still didn't reply. Andy turned around and saw that he hadn't followed him at all. He was standing on the opposite corner, like a statue.

Andy jogged back over. "What are you waiting for?" he asked. "Aren't you going to stop Gary and his friends?"

"That is none of my business," Emmet said. "I will not interfere."

"What are you talking about?" Andy said. His voice was urgent but quiet. He didn't want Gary and his friends to overhear.

"I thought you hated that bully," Andy said.

"I do not hate him," Emmet said.

Andy sighed. "But you dropped him in the mud!" he said. "Twice!"

"Yes. I did that to protect you," Emmet said.

"Right," Andy said. "So now protect that girl."

"That is none of my business," Emmet said.

Andy stared at the big new kid. Then he turned back to Gary and his friends. "If you guys don't let her go right now," he shouted, "Emmet is going to make you very sorry!"

Gary and the two other bullies exchanged a quick look. Then they grabbed the girl's bag, and ran away in the opposite direction.

Andy knew that he should make sure the girl was okay. But first, he turned to face Emmet. "What's your problem?" Andy asked.

"I have no problem," Emmet said. "It was you who lied to those boys. I was not going to make them very sorry at all. I wasn't going to do anything."

"I know," Andy said. "That's the problem." He shook his head, and then jogged over to the park. "Are you okay?" he asked. He offered his hand to help the girl up.

The girl got to her feet. Then she pushed Andy away. "Get back," she said. "I can stand up on my own, no thanks to you."

"I scared off those jerks!" Andy said.

"Oh, please," the girl said. "You spent more time arguing with your dumb friend than helping me. If you'd helped, I wouldn't be covered in mud, and they wouldn't have my book bag."

Andy looked at the girl. She really was covered in mud. Her clothes were ruined. She also had a big scrape on her knee.

"You know," the girl went on, "I've seen you and your new friend. I saw how he stood up to those bullies for you. I thought it was pretty cool. But I guess he doesn't care about stopping bullies. He just cares about protecting you."

Her face was red as she wiped some mud from it. Then, without waiting for a reply from Andy, she stomped off and ran out of the park.

Chapter 6

CREATED TO PROTECT

Andy stared at the ground as he walked home. He was so embarrassed, and so ashamed. He hadn't meant to make anything worse for that girl. But why hadn't Emmet helped? Why had he just stood there like that?

Emmet walked along next to him, but he didn't say a word. He just plodded along next to Andy as they walked toward Andy's house.

"Why didn't you help her?" Andy finally asked.

"I told you," Emmet said. "She is not my concern."

"But I am?" Andy snapped. "Why?"

"Because I was created to protect you," Emmet said.

"Created?" Andy repeated. "What are you talking about?"

Emmet didn't reply. He just kept his gaze on Andy's house as they walked up to the front door.

"Mom!" Andy said as soon as he opened the door. "You wait here," he added to Emmet.

Emmet stood in the front hall of the house and waited.

Andy walked into the kitchen. His mom leaned on the counter, looking through the mail.

"Hi, Mom," Andy said. "I brought a friend home with me today. His name is Emmet. He's new in town."

"Oh, how nice of you to make him feel welcome," his mom replied.

"So, did that package from Scott come today?" Andy asked.

"Nope," his mom said. "No packages at all were delivered today. What kind of gift is he sending, anyway?"

Andy shrugged. "I don't know," he said. "He only said, 'Did you get the gift I sent you?' I don't know what—"

Then he realized.

His mom looked up from the mail. "You don't know what, dear?" she said.

"I think I just figured out what the gift was,"
Andy said. "And I think it's standing in the front
hall right now."

Chapter 7
FIGHTING

Aug. 3

"I have to talk to Scott," Andy said. "Right now."

He and Emmet were locked in Andy's bedroom. Emmet stood next to the bed, and Andy frantically dialed Scott's cell phone number.

When Scott answered, Andy barked into the phone, "What did you do?!"

Scott said, "Huh?" There were a lot of voices in the background. It sounded like Scott was at a party or something. Wherever he was, he sure seemed to be having fun.

"The 'gift' you sent me," Andy said, trying to speak quietly. He didn't want his mother to suspect anything was wrong.

Scott laughed. "Oh, you mean Emmet," he said. "Yeah, he's a golem. Pretty cool, huh?"

Andy knew what golems were. He and Scott had read a comic book where one was created. They were the opposite of cool. They were human-like monsters, and they were really dangerous. Not to mention that creating them was like asking for evil trouble.

"Pretty cool?!" Andy said. "Scott, you created an ancient monster!"

"Oh relax," Scott said. "Anyway, listen. I'm kind of in the middle of something right now. I'll talk to you soon, okay? And stop worrying!" Scott hung up.

"Great," Andy said. He put down the phone. There was a knock on the door.

"Andy?" his mom said through the door. "Aren't you going to introduce me to your friend?"

Andy unlocked the door and opened it. His mom stood there. She wasn't smiling.

"Mom, this is Emmet," Andy said. "He just moved here from Ravens Pass."

Emmet said, "Nice to meet you," but he sounded bored.

"Nice to meet you, too," Andy's mom said. Then she turned to Andy. "Honey, I didn't just come up here to meet Emmet. I also need to speak to you right away about an email I got from the school."

"Am I in trouble?" Andy asked.

"Let's talk about it downstairs," his mom said.

"Fine," Andy said. "You wait here," he told Emmet.

Andy and his mom walked downstairs to the kitchen. "What does the email say?" Andy asked.

"It says you've been fighting," his mom replied.

"What?" Andy said. "I don't get in fights, Mom."

"Then who is Gary Burk?" his mom asked.

"He's a bully," Andy said. He sat down at the table. "He's been picking on me for a year now."

"This letter says you and a friend have been fighting with Gary and his friends," Mom said.

"It's not true," Andy said. "Emmet protected me from Gary and his bully friends yesterday. That's all that happened. I didn't fight with Gary."

His mom sighed. Andy could tell that she didn't believe him.

"How come you've never told me about this bullying before?" she asked.

Andy didn't have a good answer for that. She wouldn't understand. He shrugged.

The shrug made Mom even angrier. She raised her voice and said, "If you don't have an answer, then we can go meet with the principal tomorrow."

"Mom!" Andy said. Now he was raising his voice too. "I'm telling you, Gary is a bully! I never got in a fight. He just picked on me."

"And what about your friend Emmet?" Mom asked. She was really shouting now. "This letter says he's been in two fights in two days! Were they bullying him, too?"

Andy was too frustrated to speak. He banged his fist on the table instead.

A moment later, footsteps thundered across the ceiling. Then they thundered down the steps. Then they thundered into the kitchen.

It was Emmet.

He stomped right up to Andy's mom and put a huge hand on each of her shoulders.

"What do you think you're—" she began. But she was cut short.

Emmet lifted Andy's mom right off the floor and held her up. Her head was almost touching the kitchen ceiling.

Andy jumped to his feet. "Put her down!" he shouted.

Emmet did not put her down.

He turned his head slowly and looked at Andy.

"She was angry at you," Emmet said. "She would have harmed you."

"She's my mom," Andy said. "She was not going to hurt me. Now put her down!"

Emmet held her another moment. "If you are certain it is safe," he said. He let go of Andy's mom, and she fell to the kitchen floor in a heap.

Andy ran to her. "Mom, are you okay?" he said. His voice sounded anxious and childish.

His mom groaned and sat up. She put her hands on her head.

"Should I call for help, Mom?" Andy asked. "Are you okay?"

Emmet looked down at the two of them.

Mom didn't answer. She slowly lifted her head and looked at Andy, her eyes sad. Then she raised her face and looked up at Emmet.

Her eyes went cold and narrow.

"Give me the phone, Andy," she said. "I'm going to call the police."

"The police?" Andy repeated.

"Give me the phone," his mom said.

Andy didn't hesitate anymore. He grabbed the phone from the counter, but Emmet snatched his wrist.

"I can't let you do that, Andy," the golem said. His grip was strong—unbelievably strong.

Andy cried out in pain and let the phone fall to the floor.

Emmet scooped it up. With one hand, he squeezed the phone until it snapped and shattered. He let the pieces drop onto the counter.

"Why did you do that?" Andy asked.

"If you call the police," Emmet said, "I will not be able to protect you anymore."

Andy looked at his mom for a moment. She struggled to her feet. "I'll use the phone in the den," she said.

Emmet made a move to stop her.

"No!" Andy said. He jumped between them. "Mom, don't call the police," he added quickly.

She didn't answer right away. She just stood there, frozen. Emmet watched her, waiting for a reply.

"Okay," Andy's mom said.

"I'll handle it," Andy said. "I have an idea."

He took Emmet's elbow. "Come with me," Andy said.

Chapter 8

THE LEGEND

"Scott," Andy barked into his cell phone.

He and Emmet were walking quickly through town. They weren't going anywhere, really. He just wanted to stay away from any other people. Who knows what Emmet would think was threatening Andy? He might start attacking anyone who looked at Andy funny.

"Hey, Andy," Scott said. It still sounded like he was at a party. "Everything okay?"

"No, everything is not okay," Andy said. He covered his mouth and said quietly, "How do I destroy this golem?"

"You can't destroy a golem!" Scott said, laughing. "That's the whole point. He'll win every fight, and he'll always fight on your side. It's perfect! Gary Burk won't ever bother you again."

"The golem attacked my mom," Andy said.

"He—what?" Scott said. "Why did he do that?"

"Because she was yelling at me," Andy said. "Listen, how did you make him?"

"Um, my friend showed me," Scott said. "Or his father showed him, and then he showed me, I guess. It's like, a Ravens Pass thing. A tradition."

"But you didn't bother to find out how to stop him?" Andy asked.

"I guess I didn't think I'd ever want to stop him," Scott said.

Andy sighed. "I have to go," he said. He hung up. Then he glanced at Emmet, who was following close behind him.

"Come on," Andy said. "We have to go to the library."

* * *

"Golems," Andy said to the librarian at the reference desk. "I need to learn about golems."

"The mythical monsters?" the librarian said.

Andy glanced at Emmet. "Right, the mythical thing," he said. He rolled his eyes.

The librarian hit a few keys on her computer. "Here we go," she said. "This is the most famous golem story. A rabbi created the monster to protect the residents of a Jewish village in Prague. He made it out of clay."

"So what happened?" Andy asked.

"The golem began attacking the oppressors," she said as she scanned the screen with her eyes. "The rabbi agreed to sort of . . . deactivate the golem if the oppression stopped."

"How did he deactivate the golem?" Andy asked.

The librarian quickly scrolled to the end of the story. "It had a mark on its forehead—three Hebrew letters," she said. "He removed one letter—the first one—and the monster slept. Some say it still sleeps in that town."

"Thank you," Andy said as he stood up. "You've been very helpful."

"Um, is this for a school project?" the librarian asked.

"Nope," Andy said. "Thanks."

He hurried around the desk and took Emmet's elbow. "Let's go," Andy said.

* * *

"Lift your hair up in the front," Andy said when they got outside. He pushed up his bangs with one hand. "Like this," he said.

Emmet copied him. There was no writing on his forehead.

"Nothing," Andy said. "Now what? I have to find those letters."

"What letters?" Emmet said.

"Do you have, like, a tattoo?" Andy asked.

"I don't think so," Emmet said.

Andy sat on a bench outside the library. "I have to think," he said. "I'm not about to search your whole body for a little tattoo."

Emmet sat next to him and leaned forward. When he did, his shirt collar stretched a bit, and Andy could see the back of his neck. The letters were there, just at the base of his neck.

"The letters!" Andy said.

Emmet sat up. "Where?" he asked.

"Lean forward again," Andy said.

He used his thumb to scrape at the letter. Nothing happened. They may have been scraped into clay at some point, but now it was like trying to erase a freckle.

"So how do I remove a tattoo?" Andy said.

Just then, laughter rang out from down the block. Andy looked up. It was Gary Burk and his little gang.

Andy tapped Emmet's knee. The golem stood up. When he did, Gary and his friends stopped short, a half block away.

"This ends now," Gary shouted.

He and his two friends charged at Andy. Emmet stepped in front of Andy to block the attack. Gary hit Emmet's chest at full speed, and both of them went tumbling to the sidewalk.

Gary's two friends and Andy just stood there, watching, as the two bigger and stronger boys wrestled on the cement. Neither Gary nor Emmet seemed tired.

For a few seconds, Gary had Emmet in a headlock.

Then, an instant later, Emmet was holding Gary face-down against the sidewalk. Gary's shirt ripped at the collar.

Andy gasped.

At the base of Gary's neck was a tattoo: three Hebrew letters.

Chapter 9

GARY THE GOLEM?

"He . . . uh," Andy stammered, "he's a golem. I can't believe it."

One of Gary's friends—Evan, the one Andy and Scott used to pick on sometimes   grabbed Andy by the arm.

"What did you say?" Evan snapped.

"Gary is a golem," Andy said. "Just like Emmet is. Right?"

The other boy's mouth dropped open.

"That explains it," he said. "Oh, man. I can't believe I didn't realize it."

"Wait," Andy said. "You know about golems?"

"Yeah," Evan said. He turned to watch the golems fight. "I created Gary a year ago," he said, "with the help of a weird man in Ravens Pass."

"Why?" Andy asked.

The boy gave him a long look. "To protect me from you," Evan said, "and your friend Scott Stevens."

Andy could hardly believe it. Sure, he and Scott had picked on Evan a little, but was it so bad that he had to create a monster? Had they been that cruel?

"Scott made the new one," Andy said. "To protect me from Gary."

"I guess it could go on forever, really," Evan said.

"We have to destroy them," Andy said.

Eric nodded. "Do you know how?" he asked.

Andy sighed. "Kind of," he said. "You have to get rid of the symbols on their necks. But I can't think of how to erase the marks."

Evan reached into his back pocket. He pulled out a box cutter.

"I had a feeling I would need this eventually," he said. "I mean, in case he ever got out of hand."

"He gets out of hand all the time!" Andy said. "Your golem is the worst bully in school."

"I know," Evan said, looking at the ground. "I shouldn't have waited so long."

He slid up the blade of his box cutter and took a step toward the fighting golems.

"Wait!" Andy said. He grabbed Evan's arm. "Are you just going to slice into his neck?!"

"He's not a real person," Evan said. "What's the big deal?"

He started again to head toward the two fighting monsters, but he stopped. After a moment, he lifted up the box cutter, but then something stopped him.

"You can't do it, can you?" Andy said.

Evan shook his head. "No," he said. "I mean, Gary's been around for a while. I guess I'm kind of attached to him."

Andy grabbed the box cutter. "Watch this," he said.

Evan sneered. "Oh please," he said. "Like you'll be able to cut someone."

"You're right," Andy said. Then he yelled, "Emmet!"

The golem looked up from the fight.

Andy tossed him the box cutter, and Emmet caught it right away.

"The back of his neck," Andy called out. "Scratch out the first letter."

Emmet's eyes opened wide, like he was surprised, but only for an instant.

"Yes," he said.

Andy took a deep breath.

Quickly, Emmet grabbed Gary by the shoulders and tossed him face down on the sidewalk.

He kneeled on Gary's back. When he scratched the box cutter over Gary's skin, there was no blood.

Gary the golem had turned to clay.

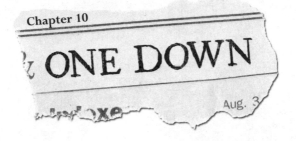

Chapter 10

ONE DOWN

Aug. 3

Andy and Evan walked over to Emmet. Gary's other friend—the third bully—had run off during the fight.

"Now what do we do?" Evan asked. "Your golem is still . . . awake."

Andy thought. "I don't know," he said. "Maybe we should send him back to Ravens Pass."

Evan shook his head. "Nope," he said. "I tried that with Gary. He wouldn't go."

"You tried it?" Andy asked.

Evan nodded. "Once I brought him all the way to Ravens Pass and left him there," he explained. "He walked back."

"Wow," Andy said.

"Yup," Evan said. "And when he got back here, he was way more dangerous than before. That's when he started picking on other kids, starting fights for no reason. I—I even started to be afraid of him, sometimes."

"There's only one solution," Andy said. "Emmet will have to do it himself."

Emmet stood over Gary's clay form. He still held the box cutter.

The living golem turned slowly to face Evan and Andy. He raised one hand and held the back of his neck.

"Please, Emmet," Andy said. He took a step toward his golem. "For everyone's safety—even mine—it's time to go to sleep."

"Who will protect you?" Emmet asked.

"He won't need protection," Evan said. "The other golem is asleep."

"Besides," Andy said. "I can protect myself. And hey, if I need help from you, I'll wake you up. Promise."

Emmet stood still for a minute, like a statue. Then, very slowly, he lifted the box cutter to the back of his neck.

Andy and Evan couldn't see the box cutter as Emmet worked, but they knew there was no blood. Right before their eyes, as he stood there—with one hand holding the box cutter behind his head—Emmet turned to clay.

ABOUT THE AUTHOR

STEVE BREZENOFF is the author of dozens of chapter books for young readers and two novels for young adults. Some of his creepiest ideas show up in dreams, so most of the Ravens Pass stories were written in his pajamas. He lives in St. Paul, Minnesota, with his wife, their son, and their hopelessly neurotic dog.

ABOUT THE ILLUSTRATOR

TOM PERCIVAL was born and raised in the wilds of Shropshire, England, a place of such remarkable natural beauty that Tom decided to sit in his room every day, drawing pictures and writing stories. But that was all a long time ago, and much has changed since then. Now, Tom lives in Bristol, England, where he sits in his room all day, drawing pictures and writing stories while his patient girlfriend, Liz, and their son, Ethan, keep him company.

GLOSSARY

APPROACHED (uh-PROHCHD)—got closer to

EXPECTING (ex-PEK-ting)—waiting for something

GOLEM (GOH-luhm)—a clay figure brought to life by magic

GOON (GOON)—a bully or a thug

HENCHMEN (HENCH-men)—a follower or supporter

INTERFERE (in-tur-FEER)—get in the way of something

MYTHICAL (MITH-ih-kuhl)—something from a folk tale or legend

OAF (OHF)—a stupid, uncultured, or clumsy person

PERSONAL (PUR-suh-nuhl)—belonging to one person

POSITIVE (POZ-ih-tiv)—sure

REVENGE (ri-VENJ)—harming someone because they harmed you

URGENT (UR-juhnt)—important

DISCUSSION QUESTIONS

1. A golem is one kind of mythical creature. Talk about other mythical creatures you've heard of.

2. In this series, Ravens Pass is a town where crazy things happen. Has anything spooky or creepy ever happened in your town? Talk about stories you know.

3. Can you think of any other explanations for the creepy things that happen in this book? Discuss your ideas.

WRITING PROMPTS

1. What happens next? Write a short story that extends this book.

2. If you created a golem to help you do something, what task would your golem assist you with?

3. Write a newspaper article describing the events in this book.

THE CROW'S

TWO BOYS OF CLAY

Everybody heard about the two weird clay statues that were found near Blue Sky Middle School over at the other end of the county. Well, they're not the only clay kids that have shown up in these parts.

John Somats from Centerville has been collecting the clay figures whenever they're found. Now, he has about 65 of the boy-shaped clay statues.

"I get calls from all over the county," he explains. And he's even gotten a few from as far away as Canada and Mexico. "Nothing from Europe or South America yet," he told me with a laugh, "but I bet it won't be long."

So what are the strange clay statues? Somats doesn't know. "At first I thought it was some kind of crazy art project," he says. "I even checked with al

EYE

the art teachers at the schools and colleges. But no one had a clue what I was talking about."

"Here's something weird," he added. "Once I got a call that there was a statue at the corner of First and Main in Ravens Pass. I drove over to check it out, but nothing was there. Later, I drove by again on my way to an errand, and found the statue. It was like someone knew it would be arriving."

Somats's latest addition.

MORE DARK TALES

WITCH MAYOR

There's a story going around that the mayor of Ravens Pass is a witch. Could it be true?

CURSES FOR SALE

Weird things happen after Jace buys an old toy car at a garage sale. Is the toy cursed?

THE SLEEPER

The old orphanage on the outskirts of Ravens Pass? It's full of aliens ready to take over the planet.

NEW IN TOWN

When Andy is threatened, a new kid protects him. But there's something very strange about the new kid in town . . .